SEREN

MARIA DE FÁTIMA SANTOS

Serendipity
By Maria de Fátima Santos

© Maria de Fátima Santos

ISBN: 978-1-912092-27-7

First published in 2024

Published by Palavro, an imprint of
the Arkbound Foundation (Publishers)

Arkbound is a social enterprise that aims to promote social inclusion, community development and artistic talent. It sponsors publications by disadvantaged authors and covers issues that engage wider social concerns. Arkbound fully embraces sustainability and environmental protection. It endeavours to use material that is renewable, recyclable or sourced from sustainable forest.

Arkbound
Rogart Street Campus
4 Rogart Street
Glasgow, G40 2AA

www.arkbound.com

SERENDIPITY

MARIA DE FÁTIMA SANTOS

palavro

PUBLISHING

Thank you to all, who knowingly or unknowingly, contributed in some way to complete the journey of this story.

I'd like to acknowledge the following people, namely:

António Zubieta Alves
Anna Gruber Bischof
Anne Mackenzie
Caro Penney
CrowdBound by Arkbound Foundation
Duncan Macintyre
Heidi Albisser Schleger
Isabel Segui
Jeanine Augier
Judith Pfiffner
Judith Kerr
Sierra Ellison
Wolfram Schleger

My acknowledgment extends as well to all the other people that also supported the publication of this book.

"If I had influence with the Good Fairy who is supposed to preside over the Christening of all children, I should ask that her gift to each child in the world be a sense of wonder so indestructible that it would last throughout life."*

In the Sense of Wonder
Rachel Carson
(May 27, 1907 - April 14, 1964)
Marine biologist and writer of *Silent Spring*

*Permission was asked from Rachel Carson Council

"A book is like a garden carried in the pocket."

Persian Proverb

CHAPTER ONE

HELGE'S HOLE

"I miss school!" exclaimed Gaia, standing by the window.

Julia, her grandmother, rose slowly from her armchair and took a few steps towards Gaia.

It was a cloudy morning. There was no sun. The sky was covered by a mantle of fog.

"My dear *wean* {a child}, it seems that this fog has been here for such a long time that I lost track of the number of days," replied the grandmother calmly.

"Not days, Grandma. For me, it feels like week after week," said the seven-year-old girl sadly.

The old lady held Gaia's hands and wrapped them on the tassels of her green woollen shawl.

"Your hands are cold, Gaia!" observed Julia.

"Come and sit on that chair with me. I am going to tell you a story that is going to take you to a faraway place, to another time...open your eyes, open your mind, and open your heart," she whispered.

The sound of those words, full of emotion, washed away Gaia's sadness. The old lady and the young girl shared a smile of wonderment.

SERENDIPITY

The grandmother continued, "Many moons ago, when we could still find traditional travellers on the roads of Scotland, the story of a little traveller girl of your age and her mother was on every one's tongue. This is going to be our story." One fine day, in the beginning of spring, when the days begin to grow longer and the grasshoppers sing, the little girl and her mother were on the road with *Barrie* {good}, an old white Shetland pony. In the middle of a forest, among the highest spruces they had ever seen, the dusk was falling quickly. Without a place to set up their tent and light a fire to warm themselves, the road ahead of them looked pretty grim.

They were surrounded by a dense forest, where the trees seemed like giants whispering and watching them. A cold breeze ran down their spines. Even their Shetland pony slowed down.

"*Thick! Nash Avree* {get moving}!" urged the mother.

"Mam, pull on the reins! Look, Barrie is tired!" cried out the little girl.

But her mother was much more worried about crossing the long avenue of trees before night fell.

"It's getting cold! Put your shawl over your shoulders," she said, kissing the forehead of her daughter, who wrapped herself up in the woollen shawl.

_ "It was like the green one I have on my shoulders, reminding us of the colour of the heather in the glens of Scotland," added the old lady. Gaia sat enthralled, listening to the story told by her grandmother.

Suddenly, a large tree came into view on the right side of the road. They headed there. The dim light seemed to enlarge the shadows of the dark green spruces.

"Who's there?" asked the little girl. "Mam, my heart is in my mouth!"

"My dear *wean* {a child}, we can't stop now. *Wheesht!* {hush! be quiet!}" ordered her mother.

As they made it along the road, they came closer to the sounds of music familiar to them.

"Mam, it's a fiddler!" exclaimed the girl with excitement.

The mother pulled the reins and stopped the cart.

"*May you raise the wind* {to earn enough to survive}!" greeted the tall smiling old man with grey hair and round spectacles, walking towards them.

"Hey! Are you folk of the *Nakens* {travellers} people?"

"You know to speak our *Cant* {the dialect spoken by the Scottish Travellers} language!" exclaimed the girl, her big brown eyes full of wonder.

"A *wee* {Scot word, little} bit! I'm a fiddler," replied the old man, taking off his woollen beret.

The mother stared at the old man and his belongings: a *cromach* {a walking stick with a curved handle} fashioned from rowan, a bag made of rags, and a fiddle.

"Where are you going?" she asked.

"I'm on my way back to my country. I've been walking for days, but when the night comes, I look for a safe place to stay," he replied. "Where are you going, *Dochters* {daughters} *of the Earth*?"

The mother put her arms around her daughter's shoulders. "We don't know where we *a're*," and asked the old man if he needed help to walk.

"I'd welcome a lift," he said. "I know of a safe place to set up a tent."

"It's fine! *In-aboot!* {a traveller expression - you come *in-aboot* from any direction and may move about greeting people at their various occupations in different parts of the encampment} We can give you a *hurl,* {a lift on the road}," offered the girl's mother.

The old man nodded, picked up his few belongings, and raised himself up on to the cart.

The cart moved off along the avenue of trees. As they moved deep in the forest, the wind was blowing stronger and stronger, causing the trees to bow to it. Then, a rock appeared with the name Helge's Hole carved on it.

"Stop here and turn to the left," directed the old man.

The old Shetland pony stopped and its ears pointed straight up.

The old man got down from the cart with the help of his walking stick. The little girl and her mother followed him.

They came close to the rock and stood in wonderment. In front of their eyes there was a hollow hidden amidst abundant vegetation, trees of various species and different heights.

They felt a warm breeze on their faces.

"It smells like spring!" cried the girl with joy.

"You're right, my dear *wean* {child}. There is a sweet scent of honeysuckle in the air," replied the mother.

"This place is a safe shelter where we can stay overnight. That path over there takes us down to the bottom. Follow me!" declared the old man.

Although it was dusk, there were points of light dancing in the air.

"They're fireflies, showing us the way," said the old man.

As they came down to Helge's Hole, they stopped in the middle of a clearing.

The little girl couldn't wait to start exploring the place. In the last glimpse of daylight, she could see the colours of the flowers growing abundantly between the trees and the grasses.

"Mam, look at those yellow *floories* {flowers}!" she exclaimed, running to a ring of daffodils growing near a rowan tree.

"There is enough space to tether Barrie. The *gloaming* {dusk, twilight} is fast approaching! And we should start to set up the *gaillie,* {a tent like a barricade, but it is a bit different in shape: it has all one height, longer and lower than a barricade}," urged the mother.

"Be a good *bairn* {child}, and come to help us collect wood for the fire." The old man lowered his head, looking for a piece of dry flat ground to set up the tent.

"Are you used to a Traveller's tent?" asked the mother, doubting if the old man would be strong enough to set up the *camp sticks* {tent poles}.

"*Aye* {Scot word, yes}, I myself came from a *gan-aboot* {a traveller} family," he replied as he helped to bring the poles, made of strong wooden sticks, and the ropes from the cart.

"The roof has to be fixed. Please, can you hold this rope for me?" he asked the girl.

"*Aye*, I can," replied the little girl, quite content to see their tent being set up so quickly.

Her mother went back to the cart, and stumbled on some stones on the ground.

"Those stones over there look to be the ideal size to put on the sheet and hold it down on the ground," she said.

"We can also use some of them to put around the campfire," added the old man.

Where did these stones come from? the mother thought to herself. *Maybe other travellers have been here before us...*As the time went by, the mother became more and more intrigued with this place, and with the old man's strange yet gentle manner.

Around the pile of wooden sticks, the little girl and the old man formed a small circle with four stones, one for each of the cardinal points: north, west, south, and east.

They kindled the fire which grew quickly and sat around it, sharing the joy of being warm.

On that night, the copper kettle filled with scented dried yellowish lime flowers, while the frying pan with seasoned oatmeal smelt of home in the warm dry air of Helge's Hole.

"This *skirlie* {seasoned fried oatmeal} tastes very good," said the old man, looking at the dancing flames.

He pulled out his fiddle, a fine instrument made of birchwood, and held it against his left shoulder. His head led the movements of his right arm playing the instrument with melodies from the Land of the Eternal Youth.

The musical notes played by the fiddler sounded to them like the most wonderful music they have ever heard. In the stillness of the starry night, they felt as if the Earth was at peace.

"Who are you, old man?" asked the girl's mother.

"I am Gazardiel, the Guardian Angel of the Secrets of Nature. I bring help to you and your daughter. At the right time, you'll understand all very, very well..." he replied, nodding.

"What do we have to understand?" asked the curious Gaia.

On that starlit night, Gazardiel was there sitting around the fire, like the storytellers of the past, sharing with a little girl and her mother the most beautiful story ever told.

Every word from Gazardiel's mouth was received in profound silence. Mother and child were so absorbed by his voice that you could hear a pin drop.

"The time I have to tell you this story is like the sand in an hourglass trickling down, down, down...," he continued. "In a faraway land, there is a Queen that rules the Land of the Young, the so called *Tír na nÓg* {Gaelic name to the Land of the Eternal Youth}. Titania has been the Queen of my people, the People of Peace, for such a long time that we have lost memory of it..."

"Where is Tir naaa oats?" interrupted the little girl.

"You make us laugh *a'thegither* {altogether}, my dear *wean* {child}," said her mother.

Gazardiel was amused by "Tir naaa Oats".

"*Nae* {no}, it's not the right spelling. Say after me: T for *tatties* {potatoes}, I for *in-aboot* {a traveller expression}, R for *reed* {a cattle pen}, *Tir*; N for *neeps* {turnips}, A for *airt* {direction}, *Na*; and N for *Nakens* {travellers}, O for *oats* and G for *grund* {ground}, *Nog*. Let's say it together: *Tír na nÓg*," explained the old man in a frank and kind way. Then he exclaimed,

"*Tír na nÓg* lies in Glen Lyon where the Sun God *Lugh* and the Creator Goddess *Cailleach* live. But our Kingdom is at great risk!"

"*Weel-awyte* {certainly}! When I was a *wean* {child} like my *dochter* {daughter}, my grandmother used to tell me many stories about a very far away kingdom, where little people could speak with animals and *floories* {flowers}. But I never believed that it really existed," said the mother.

"*Anee* {an exclamation of sorrow, pity}! Woman you have to believe that under the sun there is a right time for every single *cratur* {creature}. That's why my Queen knows that a human child, with a *hert of corn* {the salt of the earth, none better} like your daughter, has the gift to find the three children that are displaced and bring them back to their parents: the Sun God *Lugh* and the Creator Goddess *Cailleach*," revealed Gazardiel.

The old man picked up a wooden stick from the ground and sat on a stool, the stump of an old felled tree. In the clarity of the light from the fire, he started drawing a circle on the ground.

The little girl and her mother were both captivated by the movements of Gazardiel's hands. And even more by the story he was telling them.

"The Land of the Young is here," pointed out Gazardiel, drawing a mountain in the middle of the big circle. "Our Queen Titania lives in this mountain known as *Schiehallion*."

"The secret of the longevity of our Kingdom has lain in the love of creation of the Sun God *Lugh* and the Creator Goddess *Cailleach*. But, now, the cycle of creation is in peril because the Giants of the Underworld turned their backs on the Land of the Young. They took away and misplaced the three children of the Sun God *Lugh* and the *Cailleach*," he continued.

"Can I play with them?" the little girl asked.

"These children are not human children like you, *Dochter* {daughter} of the Earth. They are called Truth, Beauty and Goodness. They are three druidic stones that have to be found and placed again in the sacred valley of Glen Lyon. We just have till the 25th March, our New Year's Eve. If not, I'm afraid our Kingdom will be lost forever..." Gazardiel lowered his eyes.

Mother and daughter both felt that this story had a magic of its own; a magic that took them to another time and space.

SERENDIPITY

A cold breeze started to set in motion the green branches of the trees. They were surprised by the late hour and started to feel the tiredness of such a long day.

The old man raised his head to listen to the *souch* {a murmur of the sea, a river, the wind} of the wind. "*Dochters* {daughters} of the Earth, remember to make time, save time, while time lasts; all time is no time, when time passed. Good-night, I'll stay here near the Grandfather fire," he said.

"Good-night, Gazardiel!" replied both mother and daughter, going to sleep in their traveller tent.

Gazardiel wrapped himself in a woollen blanket and laid his head down on his bag. The ground was uncomfortable to sleep on. He thought how good it would be to lie down on a soft ground covered with moss. As soon as he had this thought, a mantle of green moss started growing under his back. He felt comforted, and it reminded him of *Tír na nÓg,* the faraway land from whence he came. His thoughts lulled him to sleep.

"Crick, crick, crick," the sound of a robin filled the dawn of a new day.

The old man was already up when the little girl came out of the tent. She started running merrily towards the ring of daffodils around the rowan tree.

In the early morning, the yellow of the flowers seemed brighter than the night before, and the little drops of dew on the grass glittered like little diamonds, she thought.

"Good morning!" greeted Gazardiel.

The girl joined the old man. "Good morning!" she replied.

"Do you see that tree over there?" asked Gazardiel, pointing out a shape engraved on the bark of a *tilia* tree growing on the edge of the old stone wall that separated Helge's Hole from the neighbouring forest.

"What are you seeing in the *airt* {direction} of that tree?" asked the girl.

"Let's go near to see it better," guided Gazardiel.

The little girl followed the old man.

They came close to the tree growing on the edge of the old stone wall and stood in awe.

"What's this?" the girl asked.

—"You see, Gaia, there was an eye in the bark of that *tilia*, and the eye was a gateway to the Land of the Young, where the four winds—north, south, west, and east—met in Helge's Hole," revealed Julia to

Gaia, who was already completely absorbed by the story.

"*Dochter* {daugther} of the Earth, put your hands over the eye drawn on the bark," said Gazardiel.

The little girl got closer to the tree. She timidly laid her small hands on the bark and closed her eyes slightly. Then, her face changed. She became blissful and started smiling.

"I feel a tingling in my fingers and a steady breathing," she said, "like the tree is breathing with me."

"Isn't it wonderful to feel the joy that comes from this tree?" observed Gazardiel, smiling at the grace of that moment.

"*Aye*, it is," replied the little girl, hugging the tree. "For a moment, I felt like I was dancing with a warm sweet breeze."

"*Dochter* {daughter} of the Earth, you're going to enter into another realm of time. In the Land of the Young, an hour is like a day, a day is like a season, and the passage of a season is like a lifetime. Child, are you willing to step into this adventure?" whispered Gazardiel.

"Am I going alone?" she asked.

"*Nae* {no}, don't be afraid. You'll never be alone. I and Barrie will be your guides along the journey ahead..." reassured Gazardiel. "Your mother will wake up from her enchanted sleep, when you return to Helge's Hole," he added.

"It's a faraway land! How are we going to get there?" the little girl asked.

"The mind's eye will take us to *Tír na nÓg!*" said Gazardiel. Just like that, he turned back and hummed softly. Barrie trotted slowly towards them, following the sound.

Then, no one ever knew how to explain what happened next: the little girl's old Shetland pony transformed into a white winged horse. And the eye of the tree opened up, forming an immense portal of light.

__"Do you believe this, Gaia?" asked her grandmother.

__"*Aweel* {well}, I believe that the tree is a gateway of wonders," replied Gaia, smiling at her grandma.

CHAPTER TWO

THE HERMITAGE FOREST

__"So, Gazardiel took the little girl and sat her on the old Shetland pony, now a winged horse. He followed her and took hold of Barrie's reins. Before a blink of an eye, they flew and passed through the gateway of wonders," the grandmother continued the story.

"We are in the Land of the Young, the land of my people, the People of Peace," said the old man with a big smile on his face.

From above, the little girl could see the glow of the trees, the lush green of the scenery, and the many rainbows visible in the various waterfalls that populated the hills in the Land of the Young.

"Hold on tight to Barrie!" ordered the old man. "We're going to the mountain called *Schiehallion*, where Queen Titania lives."

They flew and flew over lochs and fields till they got closer to a mountain in the shape of a whale's back, glittering with white and pinkish quartz. The slopes of the mountain were covered in heather and mosses that changed colour with the seasons.

They landed on the ridge of *Schiehallion*. As they got off the winged horse, a black raven with unusual blue eyes flapped his wings in the air. "Caw, caw, caw," he welcomed them as a messenger from the court of Queen Titania.

Gazardiel and the little girl both bowed to the raven. He guided them to Queen Titania through a forest canopy, where leaves and branches formed a green roof over their heads. They followed him, walking on a forest floor of mosses, ferns and lichens.

In front of them they saw a circular tree hall made of large mature oaks, sweet chestnuts and strawberry trees. The throne, made of a myriad of tiny pink and yellow flowers, glowing with a warm golden light, was right there in the heart of the hall. And seated on the throne was the most handsome woman, five and a half inches long, with long hair of the same colour as the earth, crowned with a wreath of light, with silk wings in shades of green and white, translucent like the wings of a butterfly, and a mother-of-pearl skin, dressed in green, adorned with tiny hearts and pearls in the yellow and pink flowers that adorned the dress. She was sitting on the blue petals of a large clematis flower, wrapped in golden light, the same light as her magic wand. Her expressive eyes stared deeply at Gazardiel and the girl.

The old man bowed slowly before his Queen.

"Your Majesty, here is the human child with *a hert of corn* {the salt of the earth, none better} and love by nature," he said, introducing the little girl to Queen Titania.

The girl bowed in awe. She had never dreamt of a sight like the one she was seeing before her at that moment. She could see the beauty and kindness of the Kingdom. The Queen was surrounded by an assembly of eight young ladies dressed in white, each one with a pair of translucent wings on their backs and their hair in braids of flowers. They were the People of Peace and loyal companions of their Queen Titania.

SERENDIPITY

"My people and I welcome you to the Land of the Young, *Dochter* {daughter} of the Earth," spoke the Queen. "Please, have a seat and rest from your journey."

As Queen Titania spoke, one of the ladies in white moved towards the little girl and Gazardiel with two cushions for them to sit on. But these were not common cushions. They were made from thousands of silk threads woven by Undine, the spinning fairy of the Land of the Young.

The Queen understood that they were visibly tired. She next gave orders to the ladies in white to bring nectar from flowers and serve it to the girl and to the old man.

"Who are these ladies dressed in white?" asked the little girl, turning to Gazardiel.

"In the Land of the Young we call them *Devas*," replied the old man.

"Who are *Devas*?" insisted the little girl.

"*Dochter* {daughter}of the Earth, *Devas* are good friends to be grateful for," said the old man after taking the first sip of that special drink. "I feel like all the tiredness of the world has vanished."

"How amazing is this sound!" exclaimed the little girl, surprised at the music that seemed to come from behind her.

"Cri, cri, cri, cri, cri, cri, cri, cri, cri, cri..."

She turned back, and before her very eyes there was an orchestra of crickets and grasshoppers chirping together to perform beautiful melodies. Around them there were also dragonflies and damselflies dancing in the air with an audience of robins and black redstarts perched on the trees and tweeting together.

"What a fantastic sight!" she said to herself.

After a while, the music stopped. The time was coming for the Queen to speak.

Gazardiel winked at the little girl.

"*Dochter* {daughter} of the Earth, we're very pleased that you have come to us. You took a leap forward with your love of nature and a pure heart! And we need leaps of faith to save our

Kingdom," said Queen Titania.

The little girl felt great awe before the Queen and listened to her very attentively.

"All this beauty you can see with your eyes and senses represents the external forms of our Kingdom. However, these forms are at a serious risk of dying, if we don't save the essence from whence they came. All form is born from essence. Did you know that, *Dochter* {daughter}of the Earth?" the Queen asked.

"Your Majesty, I may know that because my mother always said that I was a *fairy* {a child who shows an almost uncanny intuition about things}, a child who sees much more than most children do," answered the little girl.

"Yes, you're..." The Queen smiled. "The essence of our Kingdom is the three children of the Sun God *Lugh* and the Creator Goddess *Cailleach*. Their names are Truth, Beauty and Goodness. These children were displaced from their original home in Glen Lyon by the Giants of the Underworld. They are part of our world, but they grew too much and became the Giants of the Frosts, Winds and Storms. They are destroying our Kingdom," she continued.

Silence reigned in Titania's royal court.

"We've longed for your people, human child, to come to our Kingdom from a place of pure love for nature. Belonging and place are of the most vital importance to our existence, and we need a human child like you to bring them back home. We share the same breath of life. Because of this, the People of Peace value you very much. We give you a sense of purpose to defeat the Giants and save Truth, Beauty and Goodness," the Queen explained.

The little girl was deeply moved by what she heard.

"Where shall we go?" she asked.

"To the Hermitage Forest. Gazardiel will take you there, where an old blind bard, called Ossian, lives. He is a dear friend of the People of Peace. Tell him that you are sent by Queen Titania to help us find

Truth, Beauty and Goodness. He has a precious map that will help you on the journey ahead of you," revealed the Queen.

Gazardiel and the little girl bowed low before the Queen. "Your Majesty, we'll be back in time for *Alban Eilir* {one of the eight Celtic festivals that celebrate the spring equinox} festival," Gazardiel promised.

They rode again on the winged horse. Gazardiel pulled Barrie's head up with the bridle, leading it out of *Schiehallion.* They flew over the lowlands, the deep forests, the rivers and the mountains of the Land of the Young.

"Brr, brr, brr, I feel as cold as ice! Are we still in the Kingdom of Queen Titania?" asked the girl, shivering.

"The frozen, snow-white landscape that you're seeing is a sign that the Giants have been here before us. We need to reach the Hermitage Forest before night falls," said Gazardiel.

As they left behind the frost and snow, they could see from a distance a very tall evergreen Douglas fir.

When the winged horse got close, there was a cathedral of trees on the banks of the River Braan.

"*Dochter* {daughter} of the Earth, this is it: the Hermitage Forest," confirmed Gazardiel.

"There is a wall over there." The little girl pointed to a long row of trees growing close to each other with a line of hanging prayer flags.

"It's the wall of prayers of this sacred forest blown by the wind," Gazardiel replied.

As they landed gracefully in the Hermitage forest, lit by the gentle light of the sunset, a giant spider came to meet them.

"Fleww, fleww, fleww," neighed Barrie, frightened to death with the sight of that spider.

"*What's echt ye?*" {"What's troubling, worrying you?"} asked the girl to the winged horse.

Gazardiel knew that spider was a friendly one. He got down from the winged horse and took a few steps towards the giant spider.

"We come in Peace!" he said out loud. "Queen Titania sent us to look for Ossian."

As he spoke those words, the giant spider lowered his head and let them pass. Gazardiel moved forward, walking and holding the bridle. He led Barrie and the little girl.

SERENDIPITY

They went deep within the forest. A short distance ahead they could hear "*Splash, splash, splash,*" the sound of a thunderous waterfall. They could breathe the mist in the air as they got close to an old stone bridge across the river.

As they crossed the bridge, Gazardiel knew the way to Ossian's cave and followed a trail of stone steps set on the forest floor.

"This way is *a wee* steep slope. Hold on to Barrie!" he warned the little girl.

"What is that over there?" she asked in surprise, pointing to the entrance of a cave that, as if by magic, appeared to be illuminated by a warm glow from inside.

"We've arrived at Ossian's cave!" Gazardiel exclaimed with a broad smile on his face.

The cave was carved into a large round rock, with the entrance made of many stones put together. Moss was growing on them and the roof was covered by ferns.

Gazardiel stopped in front of the cave. "Ossian, Ossian, we've been sent by Queen Titania," he called out.

The figure of a short chubby old man, with beard of lichen, dressed in a white mantle and hood that covered his back and head, came out of the cave.

"*May the road rise up to meet you* {Irish & Scottish Celtic blessing}," he greeted them. "You and the *Dochter* {daughter} of the Earth are very welcome. Please, come in."

Although Ossian was blind, he could sense all the people, animals and plants around him.

"I can see you're coming on a winged horse. Leave the animal under this tree," he told them about an oak tree that was near the cave.

Gazardiel and the little girl gazed at a 700-year-old oak tree. It was an immense tree with branches along the whole trunk reaching for the skies, glowing in the dusk.

They bowed to the old blind bard and entered his grotto, where a warm fire and a few candles welcomed them. The soft light of the fire revealed the hard features of Ossian's face, like a face carved from stone, and the thick grey hair of the old blind bard shone like silver.

They all sat in chairs carved from soft wood near the fire. The serious face of Ossian transformed. He was smiling broadly at his visitors. Gazardiel and the little girl felt comforted by that frank and warm smile.

"On behalf of Queen Titania, we thank you for your friendly hospitality," said Gazardiel.

"Queen Titania and the People of Peace are old friends of mine. I am very honoured to receive you. I know you're on a quest for Truth, Beauty and Goodness, bringing them back to their original place," stated Ossian.

"Queen Titania told us that you can help us," said the girl timidly.

"*Dochter* {daughter} of the Earth, you're a very brave little girl, and the ancient wisdom is beyond you. Learn by heart and bring this teaching home: Truth, only the truth, and the strength of love have brought you this far. This is the power that will endure and help you to rise to the challenge of the Giants of the Underworld. When you come across any of them on your journey, send out your love to them."

"Ossian, you're saying to us that love is our means of fighting the Giants!" Gazardiel countered.

"You're a very wise guardian angel of the Land of the Young," Ossian replied, smiling at Gazardiel.

"I've made something for you that will bring you great protection and inner strength to overcome any situation seen or unseen." He pulled a wooden stick out of a lilac velvet cloth bag neatly tucked into his pocket, and put it into the little girl's hand.

"This is an *OGHAM* {the Celtic alphabet of the trees, pronounced OH-AM} stick from a branch of this mighty oak. Treasure it, keep it with you at all times, and never break it. It will forever be a part of you," he continued.

The little girl received the *OGHAM* stick with joy. "What is this letter inscribed on it?" she asked.

"The symbol stands for Duir {the letter for oak D-Duir, one of the 20 OGHAM fed or Fews}, one of the letters of the ancient *OGHAM* alphabet. When you use it, pronounce the word *DUIR* and that will bring you great protection. This is the alphabet of the trees, the alphabet of the bards and the storytellers. Bear in mind that storytellers and stories never die, because they can get closer to the heart of every *living cratur* {creature}," the old blind bard replied.

After saying this, Ossian got up and went to open a cupboard that was at the far end of the cave. He came back with a manuscript in his hands.

Gazardiel and the little girl were intrigued with the manuscript that looked as old as Ossian himself. He began to open it carefully and placed it in the centre of the table. Gazardiel and the girl leaned over the table to see what it was all about.

SERENDIPITY

"It's a very ancient map of Glen Lyon," Ossian revealed by gently manipulating the manuscript made of *Betula pendula*'s paper. "Glen Lyon is the loneliest, longest and loveliest place of our world. This map shows us where to find Truth, Beauty and Goodness. You'll fly over Loch Tay and enter Glen Lyon. Once there, you follow the River Lyon and look for a ruined castle: Carnbane castle. There you'll find what you're looking for," he went on.

Gazardiel and the little girl were mesmerized at that fantastic map.

"But the journey you have ahead of you does not end here," he said, pointing at the map. "You have to take the three children back to the Praying Hands of the Sun God *Lugh*, and the womb of the Creator Goddess *Cailleach* in the sacred valley of Glen Lyon."

"But, how will we recognise those three children?" asked the little girl.

"Once you look at them, you'll see the symbol *Huath* {the letter of the OGHAM alphabet for Hawthorn} inscribed on each of them. It's the Ogham symbol of the heart," revealed the old blind bard.

It was already late at night. The fire was still burning with wood from hawthorn sticks, offering the hottest fire known, and a cauldron boiled with soup. The smell of soup hung in the air of the cave. Outside, the dark blue of a cold night and the trees of the Hermitage were illuminated by a pale silver moonlight.

From that cauldron, they drank soup and poems...

Gazardiel and the little girl read Ossian's lips reciting words that formed a poem:

"Dream Weaving

Each breath is a movement

in the never-ending dance of the wind

a dance that repeats itself,

like a leaf swirling around

on the fragile twig of a branch.

Rivulets and the air in motion

sweep the grasses on the fields,

over and over...

as waves move in a sea of green.

In the space that leads one movement to another

between breathing in and breathing out,

there is a field, -

a Heart field

that comes alive

in your chest.

And makes you feel like

you're flying on the wings of a butterfly."

SERENDIPITY

They felt at home with Ossian, who seemed to know so much and recited words of such wisdom and beauty.

"You're going to leave early tomorrow morning. You can stay and sleep here tonight," said Ossian, pointing to a tall wooden box leaning against the grotto wall, where they could rest and sleep warmly.

The dawn of a new day came fast. In the early hours of the morning, Gazardiel and the little girl bid farewell to Ossian. They flew away on the winged horse with the moon slowly disappearing in the cold light of dawn.

CHAPTER THREE

GLEN LYON

They were heading for Glen Lyon. From above, the tall trees of the Hermitage were becoming smaller and smaller, until they were left behind in the distance.

The landscape changed dramatically below them. They were flying over a long mirror of water, where they could see many reflections on the surface.

"Look over there, it looks like a wooden vessel built on the water!" the little girl exclaimed, looking down.

"It's a crannog, a place where our ancestors used to live on Loch Tay. This is the last one that is still here. We used to have many more, but they became submerged and rest now at the bottom of this loch," said Gazardiel.

The loch's sides were a treasure trove of magnificent trees of various types and heights. The greenery contrasted with the white snow covering the peaks of the mountains around them. After flying over the mist of the loch and the snowy peaks, Gazardiel and the little girl began to be beaten by strong gusts of wind and the sound of pounding rain.

"Rat-a-tat tat, rat-a-tat tat, rat-a-tat tat, rat-a-tat tat, rat-a-tat tat, rat-a-tat tat, rat-a-tat tat."

SERENDIPITY

Barrie, the winged horse, was floating in the air with difficulty.

"Plink, plunk, ponk, plink, plunk, ponk, plink, plunk, ponk, plink, plunk, ponk, plink, plunk."

"It's hail!" cried the girl.

"It's a rain that transforms everything that it touches into ice! I'm feeling hailstones hitting my arms and hands! We have to look now for shelter!" exclaimed Gazardiel, pulling Barrie's reins. He steered the winged horse to the dense forest on the side of the loch.

They landed on the floor of a forest covered in the needles of Scots pines and other tall firs. Suddenly, a tremendous crash sounded behind them. They turned, and saw a tree with the scariest double pair of eyes and the longest and thorny branches, such as they had never seen before, coming with many arms stretched in their direction.

"Whoosh, whoosh, whoosh, whoosh, whoosh, whoosh, whoosh, whoosh, whoosh, whoosh."

The uprooted tree was moving towards them, and they could not move away fast enough.

"Brr, brr, you have to run! This is the monkey puzzle tree sent by the Giants," screamed Gazardiel. But he could not escape with his feet and hands frozen.

"I cannot leave you behind," countered the little girl.

As the Monkey Puzzle tree grasped Gazardiel with one of its thorny arms, the little girl remembered Ossian's words and the Ogham stick. She took it out and pointed it at the Monkey Puzzle tree, thinking to defeat the Giants with the power of love.

The OGHAM stick made the Monkey Puzzle tree stop, and Gazardiel was freed from its thorny arms. He fell on the ground, and the ice on his hands and feet started melting. The tree became rooted to the spot, and the thorny arms just transformed again into inoffensive branches.

The little girl was taken aback by how the OGHAM stick had worked so well to save them. She now believed in everything that the old blind bard had told her and kept the stick close to her heart.

Gazardiel was still lying down on the forest floor covered in pine needles. He was wondering how to find the way to the ruined castle that Ossian had shown them on the map, when from out of nowhere an insect landed on his forehead.

He gently moved the insect to the palm of his hand. The insect supported itself on its six legs. The old man had seen many things throughout his life, and recognised these two big red eyes in an orange red body with four long wings. The little girl bent her knees to look at it more closely.

"It's a dragonfly!" said Gazardiel, sitting next to the little girl.

"Wow!" she exclaimed.

The dragonfly did not move and appeared to be smiling at them. As soon as the girl took another step closer, he took off and began to fly in circles.

The girl helped the old man to get up. They looked on in amazement at the dragonfly's circular dance. Then he stopped and landed on Barrie's forehead.

Gazardiel and the girl understood that the dragonfly appeared to call the winged horse to follow him. They walked towards it and mounted the flying horse again. The dragonfly then led the way to Glen Lyon.

They flew above the road and the River Lyon, passing through a blizzard of whirling and falling snow. They had difficulty making their way with the strong wind whistling around them. It seemed that the Land of the Young was immersed in everlasting winter.

"Rat-a-tat tat, rat-a-tat tat, rat-a-tat tat, rat-a-tat tat, rat-a-tat tat, rat-a-tat tat, rat-a-tat tat."

They saw in the distance a high rocky outcrop formed on the side of a hill. The dragonfly began to descend in the direction of that outcrop. The winged horse followed, approaching the ruins of the imposing castle with the land falling away on three sides of the hill.

"This must be Carnbane castle!" exclaimed Gazardiel, remembering the map that Ossian had shown them.

They landed on the grounds of the castle, which was surrounded by large trees, with some of them even growing within the ruins.

Suddenly, a gust of wind hit them so hard that they had to hold on to the trunk of a tree to prevent themselves from being blown away.

"Where is the dragonfly?" cried out the little girl.

"Ah, it has gone with the wind!" said Gazardiel, thunderstruck.

The Giants were again striking at them. They started feeling too small to fight back the harshness of the snow and wind, like they were being thrown into the depths of winter. Ossian's wise words were echoing in Gazardiel's mind. In his mind's eye, he could see the three children of the Sun God *Lugh* and the Creator Goddess *Cailleach* hidden somewhere nearby. He knew from the bottom of his heart that they were experiencing one of the most definitive moments of their journey.

The little girl was trying to keep hold of the trunk of the tree. She had never felt so cold before.

She desperately wanted to stop that sharp wind.

"I still have the stick that Ossian gave me," she shouted at Gazardiel, so that he could hear her against the intimidating whistling of the wind.

"Use it now," urged Gazardiel.

"*Aye!*" exclaimed the little girl. She could barely move her frozen fingers that had turned purple by the cold wind to get the OGHAM stick out of her pocket. "*Dochter {daughter} of the Earth, remember that love is the key to defeat the Giants. Send them your love.*" The boldness of Ossian's words echoed in her mind and helped her to reach the OGHAM stick. As soon as she pointed it and uttered the word DUIR, the wind, ice and snow died away.

At that moment, the calm that always comes after the storm occurred.

When they raised their heads, a halo with faint rainbow colours appeared in the sky. Gazardiel and the little girl were speechless for a while, admiring the circle drawn around a shy sun covered by clouds.

Gazardiel knew how to read the good omens in the skies; this was one of them. He remained quiet while his gaze wandered across the ruined castle until his eyes rested on the remains of a tree trunk.

"*Dochter* {daughter} of the Earth, did you see a tree trunk over there?" he asked.

"I see a *scrunted* {a tree that is still standing but is decayed inside and covered with lichens and moss} tree," she replied.

"I believe that's what's left of a very old oak tree that split. Let's go closer to see it better," suggested Gazardiel.

They walked a few steps, but they could not go far. In front of their eyes, there it was: a wide ditch that separated them from the old oak tree trunk. They did not know who dug it, and they could not waste time looking to solve that mystery.

"The only way to get to the other side of the ditch is to fly with Barrie," considered the old man.

"I *wheeple* {to whistle} to call Barrie," said the girl, whispering to the winged horse that was right behind them.

Barrie flew over the ditch and took them closer to the old hollow tree. They got there in the blink of an eye. They looked at the trunk split into a triangular shape with a bark completely covered by a soft green moss — certainly, the result of many years of exposure to the elements.

_"Can you imagine a tree like this one?" asked Grandmother Julia to Gaia.

_ "I've never seen a tree like the one in your story, grandma," replied Gaia.

_"*Aweel* {well}, when Gazardiel and the little girl stood facing that old oak tree trunk, they bowed in admiration to it," continued Julia.

"Look at that little hole at the bottom of the trunk!"exclaimed the little girl.

"Let's go to see what's on the other side of this hole," suggested Gazardiel, kneeling down near the trunk.

The little girl followed him and knelt beside him. They looked one at a time through the small hole. They could see three little stones lying together, like a stone family, against the interior of the tree trunk.

The little girl stood up and enthusiastically went around the old oak tree. She looked in wonder at the three water-worn stones roughly shaped in human form.

Gazardiel came next. "These are the children of the Sun God *Lugh* and the Creator Goddess *Cailleach*. They're smaller than I had imagined. They're no more than 3 inches high," he estimated.

For a while, both of them stared at the mystery of that stone family.

"There is a symbol inscribed on each of the stones," observed the little girl.

"What you're seeing is the symbol of the heart – *Huath*, the name for the Hawthorn tree. As you learned, *Dochter* {daughter} of the Earth, we use the alphabet of the trees in the Land of the Young," said Gazardiel, nodding in confirmation of their discovery.

The little girl knelt on the ground by the hollow tree. She took the three small stones and carefully put each one of them in the lilac velvet cloth bag.

Gazardiel helped the little girl to stand up with Truth, Beauty and Goodness. Something changed in the air. A silence and quietness occurred, and the only sound they could hear was the pitter-patter of the girl's feet. As they took off with Barrie, a wave of joy raised their hearts up.

"Hooray! Hooray!"

They were on the way to the sacred valley of the Sun God *Lugh* and the Creator Goddess *Cailleach*. They flew over the mountains of Glen Lyon, where they could see the snow starting to melt on the snow-capped mountain peaks: it looked like someone or something had driven the deep cold winter away.

"It seems as if we're flying over a different land from the one we saw before!" exclaimed the little girl, impressed with the breathtaking brown colour of earth, the dry stone walls, and the rocks that were visible on the valley floor below them.

"This is the same Glen Lyon! What we're seeing is a good sign that spring is returning to the Land of the Young..." reckoned the old man. "Do you see the blue sky, *Dochter* {daughter} of the Earth? It'll bring the light of the Spring Equinox back to the land."

The little girl kept holding the lilac velvet bag with the three water stones close to her heart. She could feel the warmth of the sun's light on her face and arms. A sense of comfort sustained her.

"See, this is the thing about our journey; there's something else going on here. We've been guided. Now, we have to look for the Praying Hands of the Sun God *Lugh* and the womb of the Creator Goddess *Cailleach*. It's our final destination," Gazardiel said.

"Baa, baa, baaaa." From above, they spotted a black-faced highland sheep on the spur of a hill.

SERENDIPITY

As they got closer, the black-and-white ewe looked at them with the authority of a sentinel. Gazardiel knew that sheep was not a common one; in reality, it was the guardian of the sacred valley of the Sun God *Lugh* and the Creator Goddess *Cailleach*.

Gazardiel and the little girl could hear the sound of a cascade of water right below them. The flow of water down the dark rocks caused a myriad of small water fountains that splashed in all directions.

"*Wee* drops of water are hitting my face!" exclaimed the little girl.

"Mine too! Barrie has to take us to the safe *grund* {ground}," replied Gazardiel, looking down at the flowing waterfalls.

They continued to fly. Shortly, a standing stone appeared in the distance. It was not far and they headed for that.

"It looks like two large hands held together towards the sky," said the girl.

"It's the Praying Hands of the Sun God *Lugh*," confirmed Gazardiel with reverence in his voice.

Barrie landed gracefully where the standing rock stood out from all the boulders that surrounded it. Seen from the side, it seemed like giant butterfly wings, thought the little girl.

Gazardiel and the little girl dismounted from the flying horse. Around them there were still a few white spots of snow melting on the brown soil of the valley. They knelt down in front of those two huge stones, split down the middle as if they had been carved by the wind. And with great care they laid the three druidic stones at the base of the Praying Hands of the Sun God *Lugh*.

"We've had to come a long way to arrive here, but we're happy to have fulfilled the prophecy: a human child has brought back Truth, Beauty and Goodness," said Gazardiel with his face lighting up.

"Hooray, hooray! I'm very happy to meet you, Sun God *Lugh*. I would also like to meet the Creator Goddess *Cailleach*." The words came out of the little girl's mouth full of joy.

At this very moment, three transverse beams of light travelled from the Praying Hands of the Sun God *Lugh* to a hill right behind them. They turned towards the hill in the shape of the belly of a pregnant woman, now lit up by sunlight.

"It's the Creator Goddess *Cailleach*..." Gazardiel murmured.

The old man and the little girl felt great awe at the rare sight.

"Wow!" said the little girl in wonder.

It only took a few minutes till the sun reached its zenith and danced in circles, bringing the return of the warmth to the Land of the Young. It was time for the Sun God *Lugh* to be reunited with *Cailleach* and their three children.

"Today is the day to celebrate the festival of *Alban Eilir* in the kingdom of Queen Titania. We should find our way back to the mountain *Schiehallion*," instructed Gazardiel.

"Are you speaking about the New Year's eve?" asked the girl.

"*Aye*," replied the Guardian Angel of the Secrets of Nature. "It's time for us to continue our journey, *Dochter* {daughter} of the Earth."

They mounted the winged horse again and sent their last respects to the sacred valley of the Sun God *Lugh* and the Creator Goddess *Cailleach*.

Along the way, Gazardiel and the little girl were not alone. When they flew over loch Tay, a giant mirror of light from the sun, reflected on the waters of the loch, escorted them back home.

"Is this the end?" asked the little girl.

"All will be provided. All you need to do, *Dochter* {daughter} of the Earth, is to lead the way and shine your light," revealed Gazardiel.

Barrie took them on a safe flight to the whale-back mountain. They touched the ridge of *Schiehallion*, where the sunshine of the Sun God *Lugh* created one thousand tiny rainbows reflected on the mountain's white and pinkish quartz.

They followed the sound of music and laughter, echoing all over *Schiehallion*, that led them to a big bonfire in the middle of the circular tree hall of Queen Titania's throne.

It was New Year's eve in the Land of the Young, with the moonlight illuminating the forest floor.

They were greeted by a ring of eight ladies with wings dancing merrily around the bonfire with large white mushrooms, using them as parasols.

"We welcome you, Gazardiel and *Dochter* {daughter} of the Earth, to our celebration of *Alban Eilir*. Join us in our dance," invited the Queen.

"Your Majesty, we're over the moon for being here tonight to celebrate with the People of Peace. We saved Truth, Beauty and Goodness," replied the little girl.

"They are now back with their parents in the Land of the Young. And the Giants of the Underworld are reconciled with the People of Peace. We are eternally grateful to you, *Dochter* {daughter} of the Earth, and Gazardiel," acknowledged Titania.

Gazardiel joined the celebration with beautiful melodies played on his fiddle, while the little girl undertook a flowing dance with the ladies in white.

It was already late on that night of full moon when Queen Titania stopped the music and the dancing.

"*Dochter* {daughter} of the Earth, you must be very happy and very lucky! You have to return tonight to your world, to your loving mother. On behalf of the People of Peace, here is your present. But bear in mind that you cannot open it until you're back at Helge's Hole," said the Queen.

At the same time, one of the ladies in white came close and offered the little girl a small bag of white fabric sprinkled with glittery fairy dust, woven by Undine, laced with a gold ribbon, which the little girl accepted with reverence.

"From now onwards, you'll always be in my mind. You're indeed the People of Peace!" replied the little girl, looking closely at Titania.

"We have to go, *Dochter* of the Earth! The gateway that can take you back to your world is just open for tonight," urged Gazardiel.

The little girl gazed for the last time at that dream-like scene. She bowed slowly in profound reverence to the People of Peace.

Gazardiel called the winged horse and guided the little girl to the age-old crossing that separated the two worlds.

"Where are we going, Gazardiel?" asked the little girl.

"There is an ancient bridge, we call it the Packhorse Bridge. It's the gateway for you and Barrie to return to Helge's Hole," said the old man.

The little girl was thrilled to be returning to her mother, although she had left her for just one day. But she had travelled and seen so much in the Land of the Young that she started wondering for herself: "How was all that possible in such a short time?"

The winged horse landed at the side of the stone bridge with the waterfall *Allt da Ghob* directly behind them.

They got off the flying horse. Gazardiel knelt down and his face lit up with joy. He opened his arms and warmly embraced the little girl.

"*Dochter* of the Earth, this is not a goodbye! Call on us, the People of Peace, wherever or whenever you feel the call. We'll listen to you," said the Guardian Angel of the Secrets of Nature.

"Gazardiel, you're in my heart forever. I thank you for your guidance!" replied the little girl with tears running down her face.

The girl held Barrie's reins with her left hand and the small white bag in her right, and walked over the bridge. When she reached the middle, she stopped and looked back. Gazardiel was waving her goodbye.

She waved back at him and crossed the bridge to the other side. Then, she and Barrie vanished into thin air.

They were back at the same place: Helge's Hole. And Barrie went back to being the same old Shetland pony without magical wings.

"Good morning, my dear *wean* {a child}. It's just time to cook the *brose* {a kind of porridge made of uncooked oatmeal, boiling water and salted} and prepare the coffee with roasted barley for our breakfast," said the little girl's mother as she awoke from her enchanted sleep in the traveller's tent.

The little girl understood that her mother didn't remember anything about the kind old man who had guided them to Helge's Hole, and the marvellous things he told them about his own people. She was still holding the small white bag and remembered Queen Titania's words.

"Mam, Mam, look what I found in the woods!" She held out the small bag of white fabric, sprinkled with glittery fairy dust, laced with a gold ribbon.

"What's that?" her mother asked, completely taken by surprise. Then, at that magical moment, the little girl untied the lace, and by magic a vibrant garden full of colourful flowers, delicious vegetables of all kinds and singing birds nesting in fruit trees, with a fountain of fresh and crystalline water, appeared in front of their traveller's tent. Since then, the mother and her daughter have lived happily for many years in Helge's Hole.

_"Honoured and praised, my story is told," concluded Julia.

_"Grandma, did you dream this story?" asked Gaia.

_"My dear child, did we dream the story or did the story dream us? You know the answer, Gaia..." replied Julia with a smile full of tenderness.

_"I love you, Grandma," replied Gaia.

GLOSSARY OF TRAVELLER *CANT* LANGUAGE: [1]

A wee = Scot word, little, small

Airt = direction

Anee! = an exclamation of sorrow, pity

Aweel = well

Aye = Scot word, yes

Bairn = a child

Brose = a kind of a porridge made of uncooked oatmeal, boiling water and salted

Camp = a tent

Camp sticks = tent poles

Cant = the language of the traveller people in Scotland

Cratur = creatur

Dochters = daughters

Fairy = a child who sees much more than most children do, who shows an almost uncanny intuition about things

Floories = flowers

Gailie = a tent like a barricade, but it is a bit different in shape: it has all one height, longer and lower than a barricade

Gan-aboot = a traveller

Gloaming = dusk, twilight

Grund = ground

Hert = a heart

---

1   The Cant's dialect is from the book "Red Rowans and Wild Honey", Betsy Whyte, Canongate edition published 1990

Hert of Corn = the salt of the earth, none better

Hurl = a lift on the road

In-aboot = a traveller expression – you come *in-aboot* from any direction and may move about greeting people at their various occupations in different parts of the encampment

Just like that = at the exact moment, suddenly

Nae = no

Nakens = travellers

Neeps = turnips

Raise the wind = to earn enough to survive

Reed = a cattle pen

Souch = a murmur of the sea, a river, the wind, distant voices

Tatties = potatoes

Tír na Nóg = gaelic name to the Land of the Eternal Youth

Wean = a child

Weel-awyte = certainly

What's echt ye? = What's troubling, worrying you?

Wheesht = Hush! Be quiet!

Yoke = a pony and a cart

Scrunted = a scrunted tree is one that is still standing but is decayed inside and covered with moss and lichens

Wheeple = to whistle

Nash avree = get moving

Cromach = a crummock, a walking stick with a curved handle

Skirlie = seasoned fried oatmeal

A'thegither = altogether

Cratur = creatur

SILENCE REIGNED IN TITANIA'S ROYAL COURT:

*"WE'VE LONGED FOR YOUR PEOPLE, HUMAN
CHILD, TO COME TO OUR KINGDOM FROM
A PLACE OF PURE LOVE FOR NATURE.
BELONGING AND PLACE ARE OF THE MOST VITAL
IMPORTANCE TO OUR EXISTENCE, AND WE NEED
A HUMAN CHILD LIKE YOU TO BRING THEM
BACK HOME. WE SHARE THE SAME BREATH OF
LIFE. BECAUSE OF THIS, THE PEOPLE OF PEACE
VALUE YOU VERY MUCH. WE GIVE YOU A SENSE
OF PURPOSE TO DEFEAT THE GIANTS OF THE
UNDERWORLD AND SAVE TRUTH, BEAUTY AND
GOODNESS," THE QUEEN EXPLAINED.*

A NOTE ON THE AUTHOR

The author lives between Portugal and the United Kingdom. This is her debut book inspired by Celtic culture, the landscape and the people of Scotland, where she lived for some years.

Her profound interest to photograph the natural world and learn from it has been a seed of inspiration to start writing poetry and children's stories, aiming to pass on a message of love to protect our mother Earth.

The author is also deeply interested in regenerative agriculture, organic food, gardens, and forests.

She has been working in the social care sector in the UK.